the show-and-tell lion

For Emma Abercrombie Peters, Axel Abercrombie Frame,
and Grace Bernadette Frame
—B. A.

To Carrie the Lyon-Hearted, with love
—L. A. C.

Margaret K. McElderry Books
An imprint of Simon & Schuster Children's Publishing Division
1230 Avenue of the Americas, New York, New York 10020

Text copyright © 2006 by Barbara Abercrombie
Illustrations copyright © 2006 by Lynne Avril Cravath

Book design by Sonia Chaghatzbanian
The text for this book is set in Memphis.
The illustrations for this book are rendered in chalk pastel on paper, with acrylic medium.
Manufactured in Mexico
4 6 8 10 9 7 5 3

Library of Congress Cataloging-in-Publication Data
Abercrombie, Barbara.
The show-and-tell lion / Barbara Abercrombie ; illustrated by Lynne Avril Cravath.—1st ed.
p. cm.
Summary: When Matthew has nothing for show-and-tell one day,
he tells the class that he has a lion living at his house;
but when his classmates want to come and see it, he must decide what to do.
ISBN-13: 978-0-689-86408-7
ISBN-10: 0-689-86408-6 (hardcover)
[1. Honesty—Fiction. 2. Show-and-tell presentations—Fiction. 3. Imagination—Fiction.
4. Lions—Fiction. 5. Schools—Fiction.] I. Cravath, Lynne Avril, ill. II. Title.
PZ7.A1614Lar 2006
[E]—dc22
2003025304

the show-and-tell lion

Barbara Abercrombie

Illustrations by Lynne Avril Cravath

Margaret K. McElderry Books
New York London Toronto Sydney

It's Matthew's turn for show-and-tell.

He wants to tell his class something exciting, but nothing exciting has happened.

Ms. Harper is waiting. "Matthew?"

"I have a lion!" says Matthew.

"A lion!" The whole class is impressed.
"What kind of a lion?" asks Sarah.

"A baby lion," says Matthew. "He has to stay home, so I can't bring him to show."

Matthew means to tell them that it's just a story he's making up, but he can suddenly picture this lion in his head. "He sleeps in my bed at night. He purrs. The loudest purr you've ever heard."

"Matthew, don't you mean that you have a very big cat?" asks Ms. Harper.
"No, he's a lion," says Matthew.

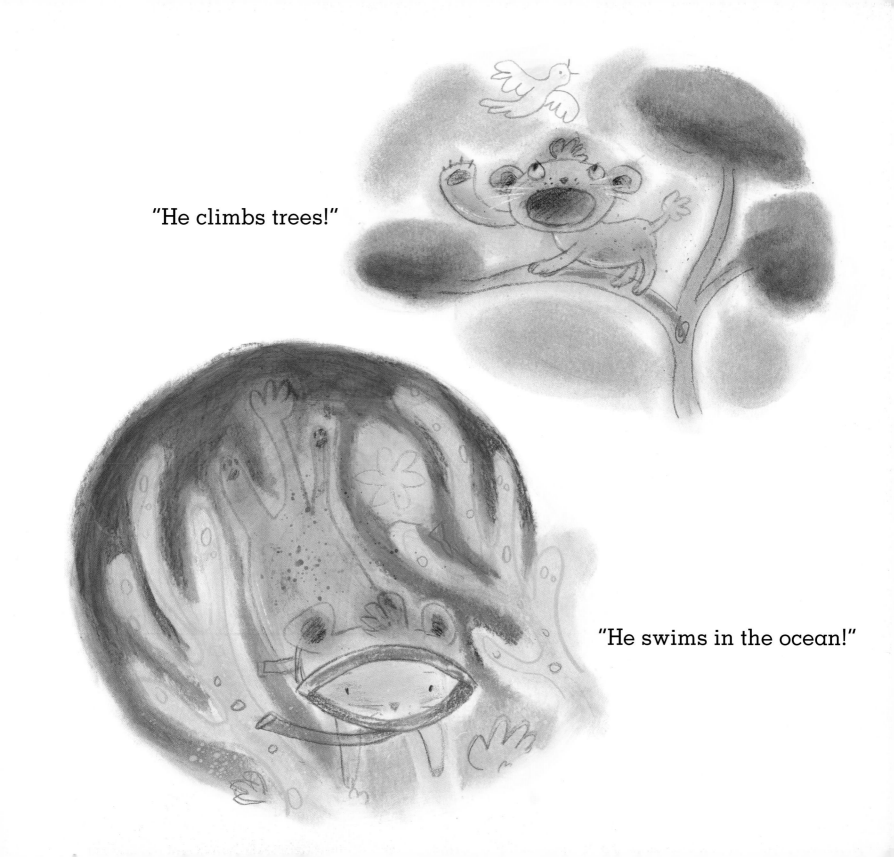

"He climbs trees!"

"He swims in the ocean!"

At recess Matthew's friends all have questions.

"What does he eat?" Rachel asks.

"Does he ever bite?" Joe wants to know.

"Where did you get him?" asks Steve.

The answers Matthew gives make the lion more real. "His name is Larry," he says.

Joe and Andrew want to come and see Larry after school.
"He's at the vet's today, having his claws cut," says Matthew.

Every day at recess the class wants to hear what Larry is doing. Matthew tells them that Larry's getting bigger and bigger. "He's almost too big to sleep on my bed now," he says.

Katie says she wants to come and visit Larry.
"He's in the mountains this week," says
Matthew. "He has to exercise. He's getting so big
that he might have to go and live at the zoo."

Joe says, "I think we should have a field trip to Matthew's house to see Larry before he goes to the zoo."

Matthew doesn't know how to
tell his class that he made up the
lion. Everybody believes him.
What's he going to do?

"A field trip to our house to see the lion?" says his mother. "What lion?"

"The one in my head," says Matthew. "His name is Larry." He tells his mother how the lion started as a little story for show-and-tell and then grew and grew, and now all of his friends think Larry is a real lion.

"You have a wonderful imagination, Matthew," she says, hugging him. "But you need to tell them that you made the lion up."

Matthew is embarrassed. His face feels red and hot when he thinks about telling all of his friends that the lion is just a story he made up. He wants to run away and hide. What's he going to do?

Then Matthew has an idea.

That afternoon he writes the story of Larry. He writes down all of the things that he told the class.

Then he draws pictures of how he imagined the lion. Larry swimming in the ocean. Larry climbing trees. Larry exercising in the mountains.

out of the tree,

then Larry went to the ~~must~~ mountains

but Larry was not afraid

The next day for show-and-tell, Matthew brings his book in. "This is my lion," he says, showing them the pictures. "He's a story."

"You *lied*?" says Sarah in a loud voice.
"You don't really have a lion living at
your house? Larry isn't real?"
"He's real in my head," says Matthew.
"He's real in my book."

The class is quiet for a long moment.
Finally, Joe says, "That's a good story."

"Matthew, will you read us your book?" asks Ms. Harper.
"Yes," says Matthew.

Now every week Matthew writes
another adventure for Larry the lion
and reads it to the class during
show-and-tell.

And it's always exciting.